Passion's Pride

Alejandro

Mahogany SilverRain

This is a work of fiction. Names, characters, places, and incidents either are the product of the author's imagination or are used fictitiously. Any resemblance to actual persons, living or dead, events, or locales is entirely coincidental.

Copyright © 2020 by Mahogany SilverRain

Passion's Pride Alejandro

Copyright © 2020 by Mahogany SilverRain

ISBN: 978-1-64786-456-9

Published by Mahogany's Place LLC
www.mahoganysilverrain.net

Table of Contents

Chapter One

Sonora, Mexico

Alejandro

A gentle wind blew as Alejandro padded on four powerful legs making his way to the edge of one of his favorite pueblos in Alamos, Sonora. His father, Gabor, the king of the La Avana shifter tribe, told him many times to avoid the humans in town, but his curiosity got the better of him. He liked watching the humans, though they were not many around usually. After his daily lessons of fighting and learning to how to rule his tribe, Alejandro revealed in his little escapades away from his father and the responsibilities of the village.

The sleepy little colonial town, known as the '*Gem of the Sierra Madre*', stood the test of time beneath the clear-blue skies. The sand-filled cobblestone streets gave way to tall buildings, cafes, hotels and a beautiful church. This time of year was the Music and Arts Festival of Dr.

Alfonso Tirado, a famous local obstetrician and artist.

Many would come from other parts of Mexico and the United States, like Arizona, New Mexico, Texas, and California. There was music, food, beautiful paintings and sculptures lined the streets, and many cultural musical celebrity guests and artists attended.

The Plaza De Armas seemed more alive during the festival, pulsing with shadow and sun, trees swaying in the wind to the beat of the excited energy that seemed to capture everyone in it's wake.

The air filled with the rich aromas of bread baking and various foods like *tamales* and *empanadas,* being prepared. The *Rosa Agave Cafe of the Hacienda de Los Santos* in particular, had the best smells and the scent intoxicated Alejandro. His golden eyes shimmered as he stopped to stretch out his broad chested eight foot long, thickly muscular body beneath a tree and yawned his powerful jaws peacefully. His tawny yellow fur with black spots that looked liked rosettes, covering most of his body on top, with white fur and black spots covering him from his under his chin to his belly. He panted lazily. It was humid as usual and the breeze was refreshing.

Alejandro had been sneaking to this spot since he was

about eight years old. His two hundred and ten pound alpha male frame throbbed and pulsed with the magical energy that surrounded Alamos. He even dismissed a tortoise a few feet away making it's way toward the town. *Even you want to go the festival, eh amigo?* He thought to himself. Though the tortoise would make a great stew, he wasn't in the mood for hunting such easy prey. He closed his eyes, relishing the energy and the breeze.

Suddenly, Alejandro hears a woman's voice in his head, *Hey, that's my bag! Let go of me!* Her voice jolts through his body, breaking his peaceful respite. His pulse sped as he opened his eyes and jumped up quickly. Was this a dream? Had he fallen asleep? Seeing nothing with his eyes, he sniffed the air and smelled nothing. It seemed so real. He wondered if she was a jaguar shifter from his pride? *No, wait, our people never venture this far and never during the day in human form!*

He closed his eyes again, letting his power wash over him. He could hear the woman's voice, taste her fear, and yet he sensed she was not a jaguar shifter, nor was she in Alamos. He concentrated a little more, seeing a beautiful and familiar, brown skinned woman with almond-shaped brown eyes, being held by a Mexican man in black jeans and snakeskin boots. There were two other men there and one was trying to steal the woman's lime green bag as she fought against her attacker in fear and frustration. Upon closer inspection of the vision, Alejandro noticed the men were not police officers and according to the sign behind them, they were in Novajoa, thirty miles away!

How is this possible? Alejandro thought to himself as his body sprang into action racing at top speed to one of the village homes. His visions were usually closer to home and mainly of those he knew. This was a first and it was like his body had a mind of its own. Before he knew it, he was outside a village home where he found a truck and he sniffed the air. Thankfully, no one was around.

He pushed the door open using his weight against it. Once inside, he slowed his breath and began to shift into human form. He grabbed some clothing he found in one of the bedrooms, black pants, brown sneakers and a t-shirt. As luck would have it, he found the keys to the dusty truck on a hook in the kitchen. He kissed the keys thanking *EL Shalam,* the jaguar god of his people, for granting him favor. All he knew was that this woman, whoever she is, is in grave danger and he needed to get to her quickly.

Chapter Two

Regina

Regina held tightly to her carry on bag, purse and bus ticket as she waited in line just outside the TAP (*Transportes Autobuses Pacifico*) bus terminal in Tucson, Arizona to board the bus heading to Sonora, Mexico. The dry heat made her sweat like she was in a sauna, and her face and neck glowed with perspiration. She was glad she used Degree deodorant, it really helped on days like this. Her curly dark brown hair was pulled back into a ponytail at the base of her neck. Her white Mexican peasant blouse with blue flowers and khaki cargo pants stuck to her skin. She wrapped her black hoodie around her waist for later. It was January, but it felt more like June. The only time it was freezing, was at night.

She was excited to get away from Tucson for a bit of fun, music, art and food. Mostly the food. She loved Mexican food, especially beef *tamales* and *cheese enchiladas*. This would be the first year that she would showcase her own photos she took in Mexico last year.

It had surprised her that her photo entitled, *Sunset In Alamos*, was chosen to be on display in the *Museo Costumbrista del Estado de Sonora*.

It was a picture of a jaguar sitting under a *Palo Verde* tree looking peaceful, its golden eyes looking into the distance as the sun set behind it with shades of purple and pink hues in the sky.

Rarely seen, especially in daylight, jaguars tend to shy away from humans. She had been hiking just outside of Alamos when she saw the jaguar sitting, softly panting under the tree. She was fortunate to have spotted one. She used the zoom lens on her camera and snapped three or four shots of the cat looking at the sun, and then it turned and seemed to look directly into the camera. She snapped the photo immediately, but she wasn't sure if it was her camera or the setting sun, because the cat's eyes glowed.

It startled her at first, thinking the jaguar was looking straight at her. She snapped a few more pictures before slowly putting the camera in her backpack. Mesmerized by the glowing eyes, she could not look away. Then she heard a voice. *Well, hello hermosa! What are you doing out here all alone?*

With her heart beating wildly in her chest, she stepped back slowly, her eyes focused on the perfectly still jaguar whose eyes locked with hers. Was she imagining things? She could understand and talk to domestic animals, the occasional cat, dog or bird; it was something she had been able to do since she was about nine years old. However, she had never been able to talk to wild animals before.

She shook her head. *Okay... I think the sun is getting to me. I need to go back to my hotel.* She thought to herself. She waited for him to say something else, but the jaguar just watched her, he didn't move or make a sound.

Regina let out a sigh. *Yeah... girl you are losing your mind.* She turned away and walked a few feet when she heard the voice again.

Hasta luego hermosa! (See you later beautiful!)

She spun to see if the cat followed or moved, but it continued to sit still, its yellow gold eyes still glowing and watching her with great curiosity. It tilted its head to one side as if studying her or even... smiling.

She thought it strange and a bit creepy. *It's probably just my imagination, right?* She gave a heavy sigh as her heartbeat slowed, the fear that initially made her want to run, now subsiding.

The result of that evening was forever captured in a beautiful picture of the jaguar. It had been risky to come in contact with such a large cat, but it was worth it and Regina looked forward to seeing her photograph in the museum.

She boarded the bus with the sign saying Alamos, but it would make a stop in Novajoa. She hoped it would not be full, and she would not have to sit next to anyone too talkative or who snored loudly. Her excitement about the trip began to wan when it took more than fifteen minutes just to board the large air conditioned bus, and she temporarily placed her lime green carry on shoulder bag on the ground at her right side. It was just to ease the tension in her neck and shoulders.

She had not noticed the deeply tanned Mexican man, Esteban Martinez, with long wavy black hair pulled into a low ponytail that stood behind her carrying a similar bag and he set his down on the ground, but on the left side. His nose was rather large, but his hazel eyes made him somewhat attractive as did his hair. His gray snakeskin boots complimented his black button down shirt and jeans. He was joined by two other Mexican men, Jalisco and Pepe

Rosales, two brothers with dark brown eyes and short black hair, dressed in button down shirts with pointed collars, jeans and cowboy boots. The three men were drug coyotes for the Carrillo Cartel in Sinaloa. They were coming back from Arizona with the money from sold product in Tucson, packed tightly in their carry on bags, one blue, one brown and one lime green. The lime green was an odd color, but Esteban liked bright colors. Each of the men were carrying five million dollars in cash in their bags. They had driven to Arizona in a bakery delivery truck from a factory in Southern Sonora.

The delivery truck held boxes of bread, sweet breads and cookies. Beneath the top layer of bread, a second false layer of bread housed the drugs. The truck also had a few boxes of coffee grounds as well to throw off the scent to the dogs if they were stopped and searched.

A regular delivery driver would drive the truck back to Sinaloa and they reasoned traveling by bus was easier for crossing the border than in a car.

As the line of bus riders moved forward, Regina reached down and picked up her bag on the left side and boarded the bus with its plush seating. She got a seat near the back with no one sitting next to her. She settled in placing her carry on bag under the seat and put her wireless headphones in her ears so she could listen to her favorite music. After a few moments, she decided to listen to one of her audio books instead.

The three Mexican men who had been behind her in line, now walked passed her and Esteban blew her a kiss. Regina cringed internally and pretended not to notice, turning up her audio book. Everything about him to her spelled trouble that she wanted no part of. They settled in and sat two rows behind her. However, Esteban decided to walk back to where Regina was sitting.

"Sexy mama, you looking good! You single baby?" He said in Spanish.

Regina sighed and ignored him lowering herself into the seat.

"Maybe she only speaks *ingles*, Esteban," Pepe teased.

"*Tu hablas espanol mija*?" Esteban shouted noticing her headphones were in her ears as other passengers looked back at them.

Regina bit her lip and groaned before yelling back in Spanish, "Yes, and I am *not* single."

She was single, but she was not about to tell him that. If she smiled, he would take it as an opening and keep hassling her.

"I don't see no ring." Esteban pointed out.

"*Aye*, leave her alone *cabron*! She's too good looking for your ugly ass, Esteban!" Jalisco said.

Esteban took off his hat and swatted at his friend. "*Callate cabron*!" (Shut up dumb ass!)

The Rosales brothers just laughed as Esteban put his hat back on and returned his attention to Regina. He leaned in, his big nose inches from hers. "How about we get to know each other better? I'm a nice guy, *tengo mucho dinero*, I take you to dinner in Alamos, eh?"

He smelled of sweat and some cologne Regina didn't recognize or like. She closed the gap between them as if she would whisper in his ear, instead she spoke in a loud, but firm voice in Spanish, "Fuck off big nose, I'm not interested!"

She leaned back and glared at him, daring him to say anything else. Everyone who heard her began to laugh, especially his two friends, Jalisco and Pepe.

Esteban stood up and sneered, "*Puta*!" (bitch!) He

winked at her and pursed his lips, sending her another air kiss, before returning to his seat. He liked feisty women, especially dark skinned ones. Her rudeness only excited him more, and he was determined to pursue her again in Alamos. It was a small town, she'd be easy to find.

Shaking her head and laughing to herself, she sat back and resumed her audio book, The A.I. Who Loved Me by Alyssa Cole. It was going to be a long trip, at least eight hours, and she was all set with a comfy seat that adjusted back and a row all to herself.

When the bus stopped in Novajoa, the driver used the intercom to tell the passengers to get off the bus with their carry on bags for a thirty minute layover. Everyone stood up and collected their things and prepared to get off the bus.

Esteban felt a bit paranoid as he stepped off the bus and noticed the Navojoa police officers with dogs sniffing the luggage bays on the bus. It was part of the random searches that the governor of Sonora insisted take place in order to fight the drug and human trafficking problem. He subconsciously patted his bag that hung from his shoulder. He noticed it felt lumpy, so he opened the bag. Much to his surprise, there was no money, just snacks, batteries, water bottles, and a blue windbreaker jacket.

"*Hijo de puta*!" He cursed and slammed the bag down. He looked around the terminal.

"*Que paso, jefe?*" Pepe asked.

"Somebody switched the bags!" Esteban sneered.

"*Como?*" Jalisco asked.

Esteban looked around the terminal frantically before spotting Regina as she came out of the ladies' room with an identical bag across her shoulders. He narrowed his eyes, "*Puta! Vamos muchachos!* Get the girl!" He pointed at Regina.

Regina looked up just in time to see the three men rushing toward her, their faces contorted in anger. She turned to run back to the bathroom searching for a police officer or security along the way. Before she could reach the bathroom, Esteban grabbed the bag, pulling her back toward him.

"Hey, that's my bag! Let go of me!" Regina yelled.

Esteban yanked the bag up over her shoulders as Pepe held her wrists. She pulled away, freeing her wrists; she stepped her right leg firmly behind Pepe's legs and twisted forcefully to the right, throwing him to the floor and knocking Esteban down along with the bag.

Jalisco grabbed her waist from behind and Regina stomped on his left instep, causing him to howl in pain. As he bent down she elbowed his nose, breaking it and blood spurted out. Before Regina could run, she heard the unmistakable sound of a gun click. People standing around screamed and scattered in all directions.

"Enough *puta*!" Esteban shouted, "You switched the bags! Who are you working for, huh?"

Before Regina could answer, a man cold-cocked Esteban from behind and he hit the ground with a thud. He looked down at Regina, "*Estas herido?* (Are you hurt?)"

His voice seemed familiar and his eyes had a golden glow. It mesmerized Regina. He was handsome with his deep-set eyes, black hair and rough beard, despite his ill-fitting clothes. She shook her head "no."

"*Buena ven conmigo.* (Good, come with me.)" He said as he held out his hand.

She placed her hand in his and felt a surge of power sweep through her body and her knees buckled. He caught her and pulling her close, he pivoted with unnatural speed just in time to kick Pepe in the head as he was trying to grab Regina from below. With a quick glance and another swift turn, he kicked Esteban's gun away from Jalisco, who was just about to fire a shot. All while holding Regina in his arms gently.

Regina couldn't help but take in his scent. He smelled of sweat and sweet musk. "Where did you come from?" Regina asked in Spanish after a few seconds.

"No time. *Vamonos, la policia viene*!" He smiled and grabbed the green bag off the floor handing it to Regina.

"Thanks for the assist, but I had him right where I wanted him." She said with a smile.

"*Claro que si, hermosa.*" (Of course you did, beautiful.) He beamed.

Hermosa? Where have I heard that before? She thought to herself. "I need to get back on the bus, my luggage..."

"Do you want to get arrested? Those men were *coyotes de drogas.*" His accent and manner made Regina smile despite what just happened.

"I can just explain to them." She reasoned.

"They were chasing you, you must have something they want." He said in English as he led Regina out the back of the terminal to the truck he 'borrowed' in Alamos.

"They were flirting with me and coming on pretty strong back in Tucson. It was nothing I couldn't handle though, maybe I just pissed them off. I mean, I don't have anything of value in my bag..." she stopped speaking and walking when she opened the bag to find it filled to the top with cash, stacks of one hundred-dollar bills. Regina gasped.

"*Que?*"

"This isn't my bag. I must have picked up theirs by mistake." She sighed.

"That's what they were looking for then. Come, I will take you to Alamos. I know the police chief. We can turn in the money to him or you can keep it."

"Wait, how do you know I am going to Alamos?"

"The festival. Why else would a North American beauty come to Mexico this time of year?"

"True, but I can't keep this money."

"They will hunt you down no matter what you do with it, so you may as well keep it, but you will be safe with me."

Somehow, Regina believed him. He was a stranger,

yet something about him was different. The way he moved, the way he spoke, and his eyes. Something about them was very familiar. *There is no way this man is human. Human eyes don't glow like that.* She thought to herself. Not to mention the power she felt when she touched him. He opened the passenger side of the truck for her.

"I'm Regina Hightower, by the way."

"*Mucho gusto* Regina, I am Alejandro."

Chapter Three

Alejandro y Regina

Alejandro drove back to Alamos deep in thought. His mind was trying to recall where he had seen this woman before and why he able to have a vision of her. She was exquisite, but she was *human*. Her brown skin looked bronze in the sunlight. Her tightly coiled hair had come undone during her fight with the drug coyotes and now blew wildly around her heart-shaped face. Alejandro could not help but notice her full soft-looking lips. He was definitely attracted to her, but there was something more. She handled herself pretty well until one of the men pulled a gun on her. He knew she had the heart of a warrior that rivaled the women in his village.

He also knew those men would find her in Alamos. She definitely stands out. He had to take her someplace safe... like home, his home. Hidden deep in the subtropical Sonoran desert. No human has ever ventured in his village, nor has one ever been invited. However, Regina was no ordinary human. She was special and it was not by accident that he had seen her in a vision. Then it hit him. *She's the photographer that took pictures of me last year!* He thought to himself.

Regina suddenly looked at Alejandro. "What did you say? I took pictures of you?"

Alejandro quickly pulled the truck to the side of the road and turned to face Regina. "I said nothing out loud. Can you hear my thoughts?"

"I... I guess I can. It usually only happens with animals though, not people and besides, I would have remembered taking *your* picture. I only took pictures of local people. Then I went hiking and spotted... a jaguar. He was sitting under a *Palo Verde* tree. So you must mean someone else unless... Wait... what *are* you?" Regina asked.

Alejandro laughed as he remembered. "I was sitting in my favorite spot and I heard your camera, so I turned to see where the noise came from and I saw *you*. I didn't want to you to be afraid, so I just watched you, *hermosa*."

Regina's eyes widened. Her pulse sped and she shook her head in disbelief. "That's what I heard in my head, *hermosa*. I thought it was my imagination. Are you saying you're a..."

"Jaguar, *si, hermosa.*" Alejandro finished her sentence as his dark brown eyes glowed to a golden yellow.

"How? Regina said weakly. It amazed her.

"It has always been so with my people. According to the elders, we were blessed by *EL Shalam,* the god of the Mayans, with the power to become jaguars. The jaguar is celebrated as it represents power, ferocity and valor to protect the land. Jaguars can see into the dark hearts of man and my gift is to see things that will happen hours, days, months, or even years before. Sometimes in dreams and sometimes when I am awake. My people have lived in the Sonoran desert for hundreds of years. So what are *you, hermosa,* surely you are more than human, how can you hear my thoughts?

"Oh I am human, trust me. I don't really know how, its a gift I inherited from my father, Abel Hightower. He was a veterinarian in Tucson. He always told me to keep my ability a secret and that animals were sacred. He believed it was our job to help others understand the plight of animals. To honor them for their sacrifice of feeding and clothing us because mankind has not only dominion on the earth, but the responsibility to take care of the earth and the animals."

"That is *fantasico, hermosa!* Your father is a wise man. He sounds very much like *mi padre.*" Alejandro smiled.

"Yes, I have always thought so too. He was tough, but fair. I miss him very much. He died a couple of years ago in a car accident. My mother also passed when I very little. My dad remarried when I was about eight years old. My stepmother, Isabel, is from Chihuahua and she has been great. She taught me to speak Spanish."

"*Lo siento mucho.* I cannot imagine losing *mis padres* at such a young age. You are a strong woman, *hermosa.* I wondered how you speak Spanish so well. A Mexican mother raised you."

Regina blushed and looked down at her hands. No one but her father ever called her beautiful. Well, Isabel did too, but the men she came across lately had been crude and vulgar. She kept to herself mostly; she was studious and quiet. She loved to read and take care of animals. Her best friend is her black and tan long-haired chihuahua, Chi-Chi, who loved to stand on her hind legs and do her version of dancing to Cumbia music.

"Thanks, so how did you learn English?" Regina said failing to conceal her shyness though Alejandro found it endearing.

"*De nada.* I learned English by watching television. I also sneak away to Alamos and other places where tourists visit and I listened to them, plus the artists and musicians who come from the United States. Are you married or have a boyfriend I need to know about, *hermosa*?

Regina felt her cheeks flush and her face felt hot. She thought she detected a note of jealousy in his voice. "No, I... I guess I haven't really made *that* a priority. Most guys tend to think I am strange because I love animals so much. I also work a lot."

"Ah... what kind of work do you do, *hermosa*?

"I am a conservationist, a member of the ACC. That's the Arizona Conservation Corps. It was Mama Izzie's idea to help me become more social at first when I was fifteen. I enjoyed the camping trips and working with the ancestral lands program so much, that I volunteered every summer until I was eighteen and they offered me a job. It was part-time while I was in college, which I completed with grants and scholarship awards from ACC and AmeriCorps. Then I went full time after graduation. I am also a veterinarian assistant at my dad's clinic on the weekends. Mama Izzie runs it now."

"You are a busy woman. It is admirable, but you need to have some fun too, yes?"

"Yes, that is why I am here for the festival and one of my pictures, *Sunset in Alamos*, is going to be on display at the museum in Alamos. It was chosen in the photo contest I entered. It's one of the pictures I took of you in jaguar form."

"*Magnifico*! I will have to check it out, but for now, I need to get you to a safe place. Those men will look for you in Alamos."

"But, I need my luggage and I have hotel reservations."

"Don't worry, you can cancel the reservation and you will not need your luggage. Those men will not look for you in my village. We have clothing, shelter and food, what more will you need?"

"I am grateful for your help, but do you have electricity?"

"Of course, we live in adobe houses. I have a television and computers, radio and indoor plumbing. We are not primitive, we're very modern, *hermosa*."

"Okay," Regina lamented and poked her bottom lip

out. She wanted *her* clothes, and *her* things, especially her hair products. She was a black woman and she hated having dry, frizzy hair.

Alejandro chuckled when he noticed her face. She was cute, even when disappointed. "We can stop on the way to pick up some things you might need. Also, there is a weak cell signal where I live *pero*, they can use your phone to track you, right?"

"You're right. I need to get a burner phone so I can at least let Mama Izzie know I am safe."

"You are very smart, *hermosa. Me gustas mas y mas.*"

Regina was liking him more and more too. She looked at him and smiled. He made her feel special and protected. Maybe he was just being nice because he found a kindred spirit in her because they both have abilities, though in her opinion, his is way cooler than hers.

"What about you, are you married?"

"Me? No, but I suppose my parents want me to marry, *pero* the girls in my village are not interested in anything outside our village. *Musica y arte, futbol, bailando, y hablando ingles*, you know?"

"*Si, pero* you snuck out to learn those things, maybe

you should have snuck them out with you."

"Oh no *hermosa*, they will not go against their fathers and I would never ask them to. My father forbids it. Let's put some gas in the truck and take it back to the owner."

"Take it back?"

"I borrowed it from a neighbor."

"I see, and does *he* know you 'borrowed' it?"

"No, *pero* I saw you were in trouble and I had to get to you."

"You saw me how?"

"In a vision."

"Interesting. Does that happen a lot?"

"Sometimes, yes."

Regina wondered what the connection was between them, but didn't want to question it too much. Never in her wildest of dreams would she have thought something like this possible. They stopped at a store and much to Regina's dismay, there were no products for her hair. So she bought aloe vera. It was a good thing she had some jars of shea and cocoa butter in her purse. They filled the truck with gas and Regina bought a burner phone, ditching her precious cell phone.

After returning the truck to a surprised but grateful farmer, Regina called Mama Izzie and let her know she made it to Alamos and she would call her tomorrow. It was a good thing she had her hiking boots on, because they had to go on foot for three miles to get to his village. The sun set quickly and Regina became cold in the night air, so she put her hoodie on.

Alejandro was quite warm as his body naturally adjusts to the temperature. He put his arm around Regina as they walked together. Her body flooded with heat from his touch and certain parts throbbed in anticipation.

Regina had never seen this part of the Sonoran desert, it was green with various plants like poppies, lupines, *palo verde* trees, cactus, and catclaw.

Alejandro could have made it home faster in jaguar form, but since Regina was human, walking is all they could do. Not that he minded the time or the company. He enjoyed their conversation and her touch. She fit nicely to his body. He was an inch taller than she was and she smelled of cocoa butter. It delighted his senses and his appreciation pushed at the zipper of his pants. He longed to make her his. She was the most interesting woman he'd ever met.

In his village, the women are taught submission and strength. His mother, however, was an alpha female who helped his father in every way. She had a mind of her own, stood up for herself and was always taking care of others.

Though Regina could be shy at times, blushing when he called her beautiful, he knew instinctively that she would make a great alpha like his mother. The problem would be that she is human, though gifted, she was not a jaguar. Still, he wanted her and was prepared to go against his father so that he could protect her. Was he worried about her keeping his secret? Not especially because she had a secret of her own.

Chapter Four

The La Avana Tribe of Mesa Esmeralda

When they were about a mile from the village, Alejandro saw a construction sign. *Future home of Groupo Susteno Plant.*

"No, no, they can't build this here, it's too close to my home."

"What's the problem? It's just a bakery plant."

"You don't understand, the bakery is just a front for the Carrillo cartel."

"Are you serious?"

"*Si*, I have been keeping any eye on them for a long time. This family has its hands in everything! There has to be a way to stop them."

Alejandro and Regina came to a river that seemed to flow from a mountain. At the foot of the mountain, Regina noticed the river flowed alongside of it. They walked around the mountain and found a waterfall at the end of the river that flowed down into a valley that looked like a lush green jungle.

"*Bienvenido a Mesa Esmeralda!*" Alejandro said proudly.

"It's incredible!" Regina gushed as Alejandro helped her down the steps on the side of the waterfall.

At the bottom of the waterfall, many people gathered to see the dark brown skinned woman that came with Alejandro. Their clothing was bright and colorful, peasant dresses and blouses on the women and bright color shorts and jeans on the men. The temperature here was warmer and Regina took off her hoodie and tried to smooth down her curly hair as much as possible. She was nervous, but Alejandro took her hand and led her through the crowd of people. Some of the children smiled and waved, she waved, smiling back at them. However, the thoughts of the jaguar shifters in Spanish filled Regina's mind all at once and she struggled to shut them out.

Who is that?

Where did he find a black woman?

Is she from a jaguar tribe?

She smells human to me. Why would he bring a human here?

So many questions filled her head that it hurt. Regina took a deep breath in and blew it out slowly to quiet her mind.

What's wrong hermosa? Alejandro thought to himself knowing she could hear his thoughts. His wished he could hear hers.

"I can hear their thoughts... All. Of. Them." She replied aloud.

Alejandro rubbed her temples and kissed her forehead. It seemed to soothe her aching head and distracted her. They continued on and the voices stopped completely when Alejandro and Regina stopped at the edge of the jungle.

A small town appeared full of pueblo and adobe houses of all sizes, a park, a market place with grocery stores, coffee shop, furniture store, a tattoo parlor, a school, a library and a church. There were no cars and everything looked to be within walking distance.

They walked down the main street and stopped just outside a six thousand square foot adobe house surrounded by an adobe wall with a wooden gate at the entrance.

Beautifully landscaped with yucca plants, white stones and cacti of various sizes gave way to sidewalks and walkways made of stone and bricks. Regina and Alejandro were followed by about three hundred of the five hundred tribe members as they made their way to the entrance.

Alejandro's father came out with his arms crossed over his broad chest. His handsome face was a mixture of disappointment and relief. His salt and pepper hair was shaved around the sides and back and longer on the top. The long part was pulled back into a ponytail at the top back of his head. His thick muscular arms gleamed in the moonlight. The tribe knelt in silent reverence of their leader. He gave Regina the slightest glance before glaring at his son who ran off and was gone so long than he had begun to worry.

"Where have you been son, and who is this woman?" He said in Spanish, his voice deep and powerful.

Regina gulped and squeezed Alejandro's hand, but stood tall and proud next to him. *Damn, he's the king's son?* She thought to herself.

"I have been in Alamos and this woman needs our help." Alejandro answered in Spanish.

"Oh my son, I am so glad you are home! Your woman is exquisite and look at her radiant skin!" Alejandro's mother said in Spanish as she came from behind his father to hug her son. She looks over Regina and smiles at her, giving her a warm hug.

"Anka! Must you always interrupt me? I was talking to *our* son!" The king bellowed in Spanish.

"And who's stopping you? I am giving my son and his wife a hug." Anka said in Spanish with a wink at Regina.

"*Oh, no soy su esposa...*" Regina began.

"*Gracias mama,*" Alejandro said cutting off Regina. "This is Regina Hightower. She is a human who can hear our thoughts in this form and our jaguar form, but she is in danger and is under my protection. Anyone who tries to harm her will answer to me!" Alejandro replied in Spanish.

Regina could not help but smile at his answer, though she wasn't too happy about him cutting her off, she understood and let it slide.

"My son has spoken! She is welcome and is now under the tribe's protection too!" King Gabor said in Spanish with a smile and obvious pride. Perhaps his son has finally listened to him and is ready to lead. He could only hope.

Alejandro turned to Regina, "These are my parents, King Gabor and Queen Anka Cadmael."

"*Mucho gusto*," Regina said with a slight bow.

The king and queen dismissed the crowd of tribe members and escorted Alejandro and Regina into the large adobe style house. It had four bedrooms and four bathrooms. Yucca plants and various cacti surrounded the home inside the gate. Mosaic tiles and wood floors inside the house gave way to the large fire place in the living room. Large windows with wooden shutters on the inside were throughout the house and the master suite had his and her bathrooms. There was a medium-sized kitchen with modern appliances like a double door refrigerator and an industrial-looking stove. A wooden dining table with hand-carved chairs with printed pillows on the seats is where Alejandro gave his parents the details of the day's events over dinner prepared by the family cook, Esperanza.

It surprised Alejandro how well they took to Regina. Especially his father, who was always pushing him to choose a bride among the tribe who would be queen when Alejandro became king.

They agreed Regina should keep the money and put it

to good use and she agreed to help stop the building of the *Groupo Susteno* Plant. If she could get the ACC to declare this land ancestral grounds, the land and the animals would be protected. Jaguars are rare, there are none in the United States and building here would displace the animals from their natural home.

Alejandro gave Regina a tour of his family home as the queen prepared a room for her. She marveled at the wrought iron candle chandeliers and the large oval tubs in the bathrooms with the mosaic tiles. There was a small fireplace in each of the master suite bathrooms. Most, if not all, of the furniture was hand-crafted. The shellacked large beams of wood supported the ceilings. In the backyard, there was a large saltwater swimming pool with a built-in Jacuzzi on the side.

When they arrived in his bedroom, Regina looked at the posters of bands and movies on the walls and spotted an acoustic guitar in the corner next to the small fireplace.

"Do you play?"

"Yes, would you like me to play something for you, *hermosa*?"

"Yes."

Alejandro picked up his guitar and motioned for Regina to sit on his king sized bed. He sat in a chair across from the bed near the fireplace and played *I Can't help Falling in Love With You*. His eyes locked with hers as he sang the song in Spanish.

When he finished, Regina's eyes were welled with tears. She wiped one that slid down her right cheek and clapped. "That was beautiful," she breathed. It was one of my father's favorite songs."

Alejandro noticed her tears and quickly put down the guitar. Rushing to her, he took her hands in his. "*Aye no, hermosa*, I didn't mean to make you sad."

"You didn't, it was just so beautiful and my father would have loved it." She whispered before quickly changing the subject. "Does no one drive here? I didn't see any cars."

"No, not really, everything is close by and in animal form, we can run very fast."

"So how do *you* know how to drive?"

"Video games." He beamed.

Regina laughed at the serious look on his face. "You are fascinating and so different from anyone I've ever met,

Alejandro."

"You too, *hermosa*."

Later that night, Regina settled into one of the bedrooms that was made up for her. It had a four poster bed and walk-closet remarkably filled with clothing in her size. A small beautifully decorated bathroom with a mosaic tiled shower was near the bed on the right side. She showered, braided her hair in a french braid and put on the chiffon blue night gown that Queen Anka left for her on the bed. It was not something she would usually wear, but her clothes were back in Alamos. Something she regretted, but with her life at stake, it was a small matter. Just as she got into bed, Alejandro knocked on the door.

"Come in."

"*Buenos noches hermosa*, do you need anything?" Alejandro's eyes glowed as he gazed at Regina. She was naturally beautiful without makeup. He longed to kiss her and hold her in his arms.

Regina swallowed hard licking her lips unconsciously at the site of Alejandro's bare chest and arms. He was only wearing a pair of blue shorts and he was barefoot. His body was lean with muscles and his tanned skin looked smooth. "No... I'm good, thanks. Why didn't you tell me you were a prince?"

Alejandro laughed softly. "If I had said I was the son of a jaguar king who lives in the desert, would you have come with me?"

"Well, when you put it that way, no."

"That is why I did not tell you *hermosa*, but I hope you will forgive me. I brought you here and now you know. I meant what I said, you are under *my* protection and I will *never* leave your side." He whispered to her as he sat on the bed. He took her hand and kissed it softly. *You are mine even if you do not know it yet.* He thought to himself knowing she would hear him.

Regina blushed and her face and body felt hot, but she forced herself to look directly into his mesmerizing eyes. Her nipples hardened, appearing through the thin material of her gown. She was not sure how to answer his thoughts, so she chose to ignore them for now.

"Thank you for saving me today. I am honored to have been the first human here. I will cherish this always. Your secret is safe with me."

"*Gracias hermosa*. I appreciate your discretion. I am sorry I told *your* secret, but only to my tribe because I wanted them to know how special you are and they will tell no one else."

"It's alright Alex. May I call you Alex or do you prefer your majesty?"

"You may call me whatever you want, *hermosa*. I hope you don't mind me calling you *hermosa* because I will not stop."

"Alex it is then, and no, I don't mind. What woman doesn't want to be called beautiful? I should get some rest now though, it's been quite a day. Good night, Alex."

Alejandro kissed her cheek softly, "Sweet dreams, *hermosa*."

Regina pulled his face to hers and kissed his lips softly and Alejandro deepened the kiss. Regina let her hands explore his arms and back as he moved from her lips to her neck causing a soft moan to escape her. *Mi hermosa now and always.* He thought to himself.

Despite her arousal, she suddenly pulled back from him.

"Did I do something wrong?" he whispered.

"No, I just... I haven't..."

"You are a virgin, *hermosa*?"

"Yes," she said pulling the covers up. "What are you smiling at?"

"I like that you are a virgin. It is not common for human women to wait. I want to be your first and only, when *you* are ready. And you, will be *mine.*"

"Wait, what? You're a virgin too?"

"Does that surprise you, *hermosa*?"

"Yes, actually."

"Our tribe is different. We do not have sex until we have chosen a mate. Some may not follow that, but most of us do. I have dated, *pero,* I never wanted to give myself to any woman unless I knew she would be mine forever. I am the son of a king, I cannot have just anyone and I want *you, hermosa.*"

Regina's face was hot again. "I want you too, Alex, *pero*, I don't know if I am good enough to be with you. I am human and you will be a king someday."

"You are more than enough for me. My parents adore you! Anything you don't know, you will learn. *En mi corazon, ya eres mia. Mi hermosa.* (In my heart, you are already mine. My beauty.)"

Alejandro gave Regina a final chaste kiss good night

and whispered in her ear, "Sweet dreams, *hermosa*."

Chapter Five

Alamos Bonito Resort

"*Estupido!* You let a woman steal my money? Where is that bitch now?" Javier Carrillo yelled through the phone.

"*Lo siento mucho, jefe*! We will find her! She was working with someone. Her luggage came to the terminal, so we know she was coming here. She has to pick it up eventually." Esteban pleaded.

"*Pinche Cabron!* You better search every hotel! Now I have to wire another five million to pay off the mayor! Find that *negrita* and the *cabron* working with her, I want them dead and my money returned or it's your ass!" Javier warned before slamming his iPhone on his desk.

"*Puta perra!* Pepe, you go to the bus terminal while Jalisco and I check the hotels." Esteban ordered.

"*Si jefe!* How's your concussion?" Pepe asked.

"Don't worry about my head *cabron*! Worry about your ass if we don't find that *puta*!

"Yes boss!"

"*Now cabron*!"

"But it's late boss..."

"Not my problem, it's the best time to get it, *si?* When

they think no one will be there! *Vamos*!" Esteban said as he shoved Pepe towards the door.

Pepe, afraid to catch a bullet, stumbled back and went out of the door. He was halfway down the hall when he realized he'd left his hotel key in the room. "*Mierda*!" He cursed in Spanish.

Esteban made a few more calls and when he was done, ten more men, mostly enforcers and mercenaries, prepared to make their way to Alamos, armed to the teeth.

Chapter Six

Carrillo Compound, Chihuahua, Mexico

Javier and his sister Rosa Carrillo, head of the deadly Carrillo Cartel, were second generation. Their late father, Francisco Bustamante Carrillo, put the cartel together in the late 70s. The cartel comprised six families and those who worked for them. They owned several legitimate businesses from restaurants, gyms, and nightclubs, to nail salons. They spread from Chihuahua, Durango, Hermosillo in southern

Sonora, down to Nuevo Leon, Vera Cruz and Oaxaca.

Javier was looking to build in northern Sonora and Baja California. The Hernandez family controlled Durango, the Hermosillo family controlled Hermosillo, Sonora, the Martinez family controlled Nuevo Leon, and the Garcia family controlled Oaxaca and Vera Cruz.

The Carrillo cartel bought stock and Rosa had a seat on the board of a corporation that comprised legitimate businessmen and women from Brazil and the United States, called the *Groupo Susteno* food company.

The corporation bought fifteen other brands which produce and distribute everything from bread, cookies and snack cakes, to heath and wellness brands, over the last ten years. They operate in thirty-three countries around the world including Africa, Asia and Europe. *Group Susteno's* annual sales reached ten billion this year.

However, the cartel's drug and human trafficking brought in up to two million dollars a day. The Carrillo family also has ties with the Azteca tribe of anaconda shape shifters, the natural rivals of the La Avana tribe of jaguars.

Twins Javier and Rosa grew up wealthy and learned to be ruthless. Abused by their father for most of their formative years after he killed their mother, Alicia, Rosa injected him with a large dose of potassium chloride when she was twenty years old. It caused him to go into cardiac arrest and he died shortly after. More deadly than her high-strung brother, Rosa is highly intelligent and a psychopath. She got a bachelor's degree and an MBA in business.

Javier is a sociopath and narcissist who only prefers the company of his sister and his two bull mastiffs, Bruno and Apollo. Rosa always cleaned up after Javier with his frequent outbursts and his "shoot first and ask questions later mentality." She was the only one who could calm her brother down and he listened to her every word. Many of the people who worked for them were more afraid of Rosa. Javier be loud and angry, but Rosa is calculating and manipulative. If she wanted you dead, you would be and you would never see it coming. She helped her brother along with their cousins, Ramon, Hector, and Josefina, to build up legitimate businesses across Chihuahua. They made Chihuahua one of the most dangerous states in Mexico with the highest murder count.

They owned their father's sprawling Californian 1940s Colonial style home on twenty acres. Impeccably preserved with its stone, mosaics, wood, stained glass ceiling in the foyer and windows in the master bath, stave and marble floors, high ceilings, and ornate wrought iron design on the staircase and patio railings, it is an architectural jewel. Six bedrooms and seven and a half bathooms with a central hall two levels high with a lamp and a chimney made of pink quarry. From there, you have access to the living room, dining room, kitchen, the study, (which is Javier and Rosa's office), living room and service areas.

Through the main staircase you have access to the basement where there is a game room or you can go up to the upper floor where there is the private area that consists of a master bedroom that Javier and Rosa shared with a large living room and dressing room made of fine wood and a double bathroom with a sauna. If anyone thought it odd that they shared a bedroom, they kept their comments to themselves or came up missing.

Another bedroom with a dressing room and bathroom, three more had walk-in closets and one bedroom has a terrace. The third level has a gym/yoga room with stave floors and panoramic views. Javier wanted to sell it after their father died, but Rosa insisted they keep it, having it redecorated and maintaining its upkeep.

Javier slammed his white iPhone on the marble desk in his home office.

"*Que paso hermano*?" Rosa asked.

"Those *estupido idiotas,* Esteban and his crew lost

five million of the fifteen that was going to Alamos to some *Americana negrita* and a *Mexicano cabron* who Esteban says is not human!"

"*Calmate mi amor.* I will call Culebra to see if the man is from his tribe, but I doubt that anyone from his tribe is involved. We give them more than enough to keep them happy. *Pero*, he may know of another tribe."

"*Mierda*! There is more than one tribe of snakes?"

"No, Javier, not snakes, jaguars."

"Since when?"

"Since forever, but they have never interfered before."

"How do you know this?"

"I make it my business to know as much as I can so no one stands in our way." Rosa said coldly.

Javier walked over to Rosa and pulling her to a standing position, he cupped her ass and kissed her deeply.

"That is why I love you, you always take care of everything. I don't know what I would do without you." He whispered.

"Don't worry *mi amor,* I will handle this." She whispered back, kissing him again softly.

Chapter Seven

Nuevo Guaymas, San Carlos
Culebra

Salvador "*Culebra*" Hermosillo was the twenty-seven- year old nephew of Juan Pablo Hermosillo, head of the Hermosillo family in southern Sonora. His father, Izan, married into the Azteca tribe of anaconda shape shifters.

Culebra took after his beautiful mother, Atzi. Being a

half-breed shifter was not so unusual. However, it had one side effect for Culebra. One of his eyes was yellow with the slit pupil of a snake at birth, giving him a unique appearance. Despite his eyes, he is handsome, light brown skinned with shoulder length black hair, and a strong jaw.

He looks more Native American than Mexican, but his snake eye makes most people uncomfortable, even the tribe members. He prefers staying with his mother in their village near San Carlos in Nuevo Guaymas, eighty-five miles from Hermosillo.

Six months ago, he met a feisty woman on the beach in San Carlos, Yolanda Greene from California. She was a beautiful curvy African American woman with shoulder length locs in her 30s. She didn't mind his snake eye as she loves snakes, having a Mexican boa named *Sancho*, and several smaller ones as pets. She also has a snake tattoo around her left ankle. She and Culebra became inseparable.

Jolted out of a peaceful slumber by his phone, he picks it up and seeing that it is Rosa Carrillo, he answers, "*Hola*." His voice deep and hoarse from sleep.

"Culebra, we have a problem. Esteban's crew was taken for five million by a man with supernatural ability and a young black woman from Arizona. Does that sound like someone from your tribe?" Rosa asked.

"No boss lady, no American black women in my tribe from Arizona. Not that they aren't some fine ass looking women, though. *Pero*, could be La Avana tribe. Me and my crew will go to Alamos tomorrow and check it out." He said with a quick glance at Yolanda who lay peacefully at his side.

"*Gracias*, if you find them, you know what to do and keep the *dinero*. Consider it payment for services rendered."

"*Muchas gracias, jefa*!" Culebra said before hanging up.

Yolanda stirred in bed next to him. He leans over and kisses her round bare bottom and playfully smacks it.

"Boy stop, you play too much!" She laughs as he turns her over and pulling her up to a sitting position, kisses her. She hugged his neck, wrapping her legs around his waist and smooths his long hair behind his ears. "You think she's onto us?" She asks nervously.

"No Yolanda, if she knew we've been skimming, we'd be dead already. Apparently, there is *another* black woman who stole five million from Esteban."

"Now that's a whole lotta green baby, more than our chump change! Does Rosa know who?"

"No, but if she is with the La Avana tribe, she won't

be hard to find and the money is ours to keep."

"Hell, let's get the fuck on then!" Yolanda got up.

"Oh no, that can wait until morning! Just looking at your naked ass makes my dick hard."

"Oh, ok then, lemme take care of that right now!" She said as she slid her hands down his chest and pushes him back onto the bed. Yolanda kisses her way down his chiseled chest, hiking her plump bottom up in the air.

Culebra eyed her lustfully as she continued her onslaught of kisses until she reaches his already throbbing thick member. Taking it in her hands, She licks the base along the pulsing thick vein up to the tip before sliding it in her warm mouth until it reaches the back of her throat. Sliding it in and out of her mouth, she worked as her right hand slid down to cup his balls.

Culebra threw his head back against the pillow. "Damn baby," he hissed. When he couldn't stand it any longer, he pulled her by the hair. "Get on your knees,"he commands.

She quickly obeys. He got up on his knees and smacks her ass several times forcing a squeal of delight from her. He grabbed a condom from the nightstand, ripped it open and quickly slid it on before thrusting himself into her, pulling back and thrusting deeper. She moans and slams her body back against him.

"Yes, baby!" she cried.

He began to slam harder and faster. "Whose pussy is this?" he demanded.

"Yours baby," she moaned just before a delicious wave slammed into her and she spilled her essence. Her body shook as his power spread over her body. She trembled as the next wave of pleasure consumed her.

Culebra pulled out and flipping her onto her back, pulling her legs around his shoulders, he plunged between her legs at an inhuman speed. His eyes began to glow as he hisses on the verge of release. With one final thrust he releases powerfully. Their bodies trembling together as his power washes over them.

Yolanda opened her eyes, they glowed a honey brown. This was always the most exciting part for her. His power made every nerve in her body tingle. She loved every minute. She would remain on a high for a few more minutes as Culebra slid out and removed the condom. Then he placed her legs gently on the bed. She panted softly as he slid her legs open and using his forked tongue, he licked and feasted on her until another orgasm caused her to spill her essence again.

"Culebra, *te quiero mucho,*" she breathes.

Swallowing every drop, he gently closed her legs and slithered up her body kissing as he went until he hovered over her neck and whispers, "I love you very much too, *mi amor*."

Chapter Eight

Alejandro's Vision

"No, no, noo!"Alejandro woke with a start in a cold sweat. He had another vision. This time of his village.

Regina and his parents rushed to his room.

"*Que pasa hijo?*" Gabor was the first to speak.

"*Ellos vienen, papa.* (They're coming, papa.)" Alejandro said wearily.

"*Aqui?*" Anka asked.

"*Si mama.*"

"The *coyotes*, but how?" Regina asked.

"I don't think so, *hermosa*. Maybe cartel enforcers and I saw an Aztecta too.

"*Aye no! Por que?*" his mother gasped.

"*Yo no se, mama.*"

"Who are the Aztecas?" Regina asked in English as she sat next to him on the bed.

Alejandro touches her face lovingly. "They are another shifter tribe like ours, *pero*, they are snakes, yellow anacondas."

Damn, not snakes! Just how many different shifters are there? Regina thought.

"Oh no, snakes are the only animals I do not get along with. They are cold blooded by nature and they spook easily."

"You can talk to snakes too?" Queen Anka asked Regina in Spanish.

"Yes, but they give me the creeps!" Regina answered in Spanish and laughed.

King Gabor stormed out of the room to prepare the men to fight.

"When are they coming Alex?" Regina asked in English.

"Maybe today or tomorrow, I just saw them fighting, I need to go with *mi padre*."

"Mama, can Regina stay with you and the children of the tribe?" Alejandro asked in Spanish.

"No, Alex, I can fight, my father trained me in hand-to-hand combat." Regina interjected in English.

"That may be so, but they are not *human*, Regina! Once an anaconda wraps around you, they will crush you. They can do that in their human form too. Besides, I need you to protect my mother and the children, please *hermosa*." He pleads in English.

It was the first time he called her by her given name and reading his thoughts; she knew he had seen his mother die. She would do whatever he needed her to do. "Okay, I will."

"*Gracias, hermosa*!" Alejandro said as he kissed her forehead and his mother's cheek before rushing after his father.

"What's happening, daughter? I don't have to read your mind to know you heard my son's thoughts." Anka said in Spanish as she folded her arms, her eyes searching Regina for answers. Stubborn and determined, Regina knew she was no match for his mother. Yet, it tore her. She was not sure she should say anything, but she knew Anka would not stop pressing her for answers.

"He saw you die." Regina said sadly in Spanish.

"I see. Well, let's go then." Anka answered in Spanish, sighing heavily.

The women left Alejandro's bedroom, dressed, ate breakfast and went to the homes of tribe members, rounding up the children and those too old or ill to fight. Queen Anka led them all to the built-in hiding place in the church.

*****

Yolanda held on tight to Culebra as they rode on his black Harley Davidson Electra Glide with custom painted yellow anaconda on the side. Behind them was twenty-five of his toughest tribe members on their custom painted bikes, eight of whom were women. It was a three hour ride to Alamos then another twenty-five minutes to *Mesa Esmeralda.*

Culebra had not been out this way in three years. Though the La Avana tribe kept to themselves mostly, a rival hundreds of years old existed between them. However, Culebra, like Alejandro, used to sneak away from his tribe. They came across each other in the desert as children, but instead of fighting, they became friends.

Alejandro was two years older and every few months or so, they would meet up and either race or playfully compete in whatever their minds would come up with. Alejandro was the first to accept Culebra and not be cruel to him like some of his tribal brothers about his unusual appearance calling him "half-breed" and such.

Culebra had to fight to earn his place in the tribe. He had done so three years ago when he started working for the Carrillo Cartel through his uncle, Juan Pablo. His exploits garnered favors and a source of revenue for the tribe. He stopped coming to the desert to meet with Alejandro as his popularity within the tribe grew. He never explained to Alejandro why he stopped coming and now, he would have to face him. He would have to betray his only real friend, save for Yolanda, to get the five million. He lied to his crew saying it was a million dollars he was after.

His plan was to ditch his crew in Alamos and meet with Alejandro first, get the money and fake the deaths of the girl and whatever tribe member helped her. Send the proof to Rosa, give his tribe one million and he and Yolanda would leave with four million and never look back. No blood shed for either side. However, it all hinged on whether Alejandro still considered him a friend.

When the Aztecas arrived in Alamos at the *Rosa Agave Cafe of the Hacienda De Los Santos* to get food and fuel, Esteban was waiting with his crew of mercenaries and loyal soldiers.

Fucking hell! Culebra hissed to himself. Esteban and the men with him stuck out like sore thumbs amid the festival attendees.

Esteban walked over to Culebra as he, Yolanda and the others got off their bikes.

"Culebra, good to see you!" Esteban gave a fake

smile.

"Esteban." Culebra hissed.

"Rosa told me you know where to find this *cabron* and that *pinche puta*!"

"I have an idea, *pero*, I wanted to do some recon first. Rosa told me the *dinero* is mine to keep for services rendered."

"I don't care about that, I just want the girl *alive, entiendes*?"

"*Claro que si*. So what's with them?" Culera nodded to the menacing looking men behind Esteban.

"Back up, for that *cabron*! He's not human! Rosa says he is like *your* tribe."

"*Si*, something like that."

"What's with them?" Esteban pointed to the bikers with Culebra.
"Back up, just in case. Gotta stay prepared, man."

"*Bueno*, can't be too careful." Esteban agreed as Yolanda caught his eye. He stepped closer. "She yours?"

Culebra possessively stepped between them, sliding Yolanda behind him.

"Yes." Culebra hissed. Yolanda just glared at Esteban.

Esteban threw up his hands. "Okay, okay. She's a foxy lady, though!" *Another feisty black woman, lucky bastard.* He thought to himself.

"We're gonna refuel and eat. Then I'm gonna head out to see if I can find the *exacto* location. When I've got it, I'll come back here and we can all go, got it?" Culebra hissed. "*Solo?*"

"No, my woman is coming with me."

"*Puede ella pelear?*"

Yolanda bucked, "Can I fight? Mutha fucka, I'll kick yo big nose ass right here!"

"*Tranquila mi amor*, no need for that. We're on the same side, right?" Culebra touched her hand as he looked at Esteban. His touch calmed her, but she didn't trust Esteban and told Culebra as much.

"She speaks Spanish, too? *Perfecto!*" Esteban chuckled. He knew she meant it. *Too bad she belongs to that snake-eyed cabron.*

"Another time, *eh mujer?*" He said as he licked his lips staring lustfully at Yolanda.

Culebra was trying to keep his cool so he let that last remark slide. "You joining us?" Culebra pointed to the restaurant.

"No, you go ahead, we'll be at the Alamos Bonito Resort. Text me when you get back." Esteban handed a card to Culebra.

"*Bueno*." Culebra took the card and he and his crew went inside to eat.

One of the American mercenaries came up to Esteban. "You want me to follow him?"

"*Si*, and take the others with you. Kill him and the other two targets, bring the money and *his* woman back to me."

"You got it."

Chapter Nine

Mesa Esmeralda

Alejandro. A familiar voice in his head grabbed his attention and he closed his eyes. *Culebra?*

He began to see Culebra and a woman on his Harley heading to the village. He looked troubled. Though Alejandro had not spoken to him in three years, he still considered him a friend. A friend that seemed to need his help now. Alejandro immediately made his way to the waterfall.

By the time he made his way to the river on the other side of the mountain, he could see them in the distance along with the cloud of sand behind them.

Culebra spotted someone by the mountain, he really had not been sure exactly where the village was until now. As got closer, he recognized Alejandro.

He knew I was coming. Culebra thought to himself.

He had almost forgotten about Alejandro's visions of the future. He would know about Culebra coming. Since Alejandro was alone, it meant no one had to get hurt. Culebra smiled, thankful that this would go easier than he thought.

He stopped about five feet away, telling Yolanda to "stay put" on the bike until he returned. She was about to protest, but one look at Culebra's face told her it was not the time to argue.

"Alejandro, *mi amigo*. It's good to see you! I wish I had good news." Culebra shook his hand and Alejandro pulled him in for a brotherly hug.

Culebra felt the warmth and friendship flow between and a tear slid from his snake eye. "*Amigo, lo siento mucho. I know the girl is here, I don't mean you or her any harm. I just need the dinero*."

"You work for the cartel *hermano*? That's why I haven't seen you?"

"Yeah. I don't deserve to be called *hermano*. I was just trying to survive, man. I didn't fit in anywhere. I would always be..."

"An outsider. No apology needed, *mi hermano*. I will give you what you need, though it looks like you have found someone who doesn't see you as an outsider."

Alejandro nodded in Yolanda's direction.

"*Si, si. Pero you* never treated me like an outsider either."

"Alejandro, who is this man?" King Gabor asked in Spanish from behind Alejandro.

Alejandro spun to see his father and several of the tribe members behind him. "*Papa, este es mi amigo y mi hermano, Salvador Culebra Hermosillo.*" Alejandro said.

King Gabor looked Culebra over. "*Es un Azteca!? Por que?*"

Suddenly, Yolanda heard the familiar sounds of bikes and cars coming fast. "Culebra, They're here! *Vamos!*"

"*Mierda!* They must have tracked me! *Lo siento!* You and your people go back, Alejandro. I will deal with them!"

"If they are here, they know you betrayed them. They will kill you and your woman. I will fight with you!"

"What happened son? Did your "friend" betray you?" King Gabor asked in Spanish.

"No, father, he betrayed them!" Alejandro shouted in Spanish pointing to the cloud of dust coming their way.

Culebra motioned for Yolanda to come to him. "Oh hell no, I'm not staying here, let's go Culebra!"

"If we run now, they will hunt us down and kill us! Those men are killers for hire." Culebra explained.

Alejandro shouted in Spanish for one of his tribe members to take Yolanda to his mother and Regina inside the village. Yolanda looked to Culebra and he nodded. "Go, be safe, I will come for you when this is over. *Te quiero!*"

Yolanda ran to Culebra throwing her arms around him. "You betta make sure yo ass comes back, you hear me?" She threatened. He kissed her, then shoved her away mouthing the word, "go."

Tears streaming down her face, she headed to the village.

"We fight together then!" King Gabor shouted in Spanish, proud to fight by his son's side. They were not too far away now, but closing in fast.

"None of my tribe is with them." Culebra said.

"No, they are here to kill *us*. *Pero*, they are only human!" Alejandro said with a wink as more of his tribe members came from the mountain. At least ten more men joined them as they waited for the killers to arrive.

The mercenaries and enforcers stopped a few feet away. The ring leader, known as Acid Drip, a blue-eyed blonde ex special ops guy turned mercenary, stepped forward.

"Culebra, I knew you were a traitor! No matter, give us the money and the girl, and I will spare your lives!"

"Not a chance, *hombre*!" Culebra said.

"Leave now and we will spare *your* lives!" Alejandro countered.

On King Gabor's signal, the warriors charged the nine visible men and the shooting began. The warriors were hit, but they kept coming. The bullets came out almost as quickly as they went in. The tribe quickly overwhelmed the human men, slashing them with their claws. The humans threw down their guns and pulled out knives. Culebra seemed to move through the fray with ease, his eyes set on Acid Drip, so he didn't notice the knife that was about to pierce his side.

Alejandro saw it and sprang into jaguar form, tackling the man to the ground before opening his jaws, and with two hundred pounds of pressure, he bit the back of his head. He pierced the skull, killing the man instantly.

Culebra gave a quick nod to Alejandro and continued to make his way to Acid Drip.

Alejandro was suddenly hit with a vision. There was one man hiding behind one of the black SUVs. He loaded his rifle with silver bullets and set his sights on the king. Alejandro snapped to and raced to the SUV. He jumped the man, knocking him to the ground, but not before he took a shot that hit King Gabor between the eyes and he fell to the ground.

Alejandro roared and slashed the man's throat, leaving him to bled out. He raced back to his father. "No, no, noo!" He cried.

Culebra, who had just crushed Acid Drip in his arms, dropped him and spun to see Alejandro and several tribe members weeping over the dead king. Culebra rushed to him.

"*Hermano*, get your father back to the village. I will call my crew to dispose of the bodies."

"No, then they will know you helped us." Alejandro said tearfully. Then he stood and ordered four men to help him carry his father home. The rest were to stay and help Culebra dispose of the bodies and the cars. "When you're done, your woman and your money will be waiting for you, *hermano. Mi hermosa* didn't want it anyway."

"Wait, the girl is yours? Why did she steal it?"

"She is and it was an accident, she picked up the wrong bag."

"Damn bro, I didn't know that. We have good taste in women! It's a shame she was about to die over a misunderstanding. You keep it Alejandro, you have suffered enough. I will take Yolanda home."

"No, it will help free you, *hermano*. You won't need

the cartel and neither will your people."

"*Gracias*, I will tell my father and my uncle how Rosa Carrillo put a hit on me and you saved my life. We will have no quarrel with you after this, I am sure. I'm sorry about your dad. Will you be the new king?"

"*Si hermano*, now go. I need to tend to my father's funeral arrangements and my mother's grief."

Culebra knelt before Alejandro and the other tribe members did the same.

Chapter Ten

King Alejandro

Two days after the fight, Culebra and Yolanda returned to *Mesa Esmeralda* for King Gabor's funeral. Everyone wore death masks and dressed in white as usually done with the death of a royal. They placed King Gabor on a pyre at the church. Alejandro, holding Regina's hand, and his mother, Queen Anka, led the procession of five hundred people through the town to the church. Culebra, Yolanda, his parents and maternal grandfather, were special guests.

The high priest said a few words before stepping back to allow each tribe member and guest to place a flower, corn, or any gift they wanted to send with Gabor. After everyone said their goodbyes, the priest set the body ablaze. Smoke and ash ascended to the heavens.

After the funeral, Alejandro and Queen Anka met with Culebra's parents and grandfather, Chimalli, the Azteca Anaconda king in his parent's home.

For the first time in a hundred years, they signed a peace agreement between the two tribes.

While the peace agreement was being signed, many of the tribe members began to prepare for Alejandro's coronation in a few days. Regina, Culebra and Yolanda sat in the living room.

"So Regina girl, when is your wedding? I wanna make sure we come back for that!" Yolanda asked.

Everything happened so fast, the last few days became a blur. She and Yolanda bonded a couple days ago when the village was under attack. Regina was unsure if she wanted to get married. Sure, she was pushing thirty, but she had a job she loved, Mama Izzie and Chi-Chi, her two-year-old long-haired chihuahua. Besides, Alejandro said she was his, but he didn't officially ask her to marry him. She supposed if he did, she could put in for a transfer to Mexico. She could bring Chi-Chi here and still visit Mama Izzie every couple of months.

"Well, with everything going on, I mean, Alejandro and I just met, he needs time to grieve, his coronation is coming up..."

"Hmph, excuses! Only a fool couldn't see that man is crazy about you! I'm sure he'll ask soon. Don't you want to be queen? If I was you, I'd jump on that honey!"

Culebra hissed and arched his eyebrow over his snake-eye.

"Baby, you know I'm *yo* woman! I said *if* I was *her*. Anywayze... what have you got to lose? The sex ain't good or sumpthin?"

Regina's cheeks flushed with embarrassment and she smoothed out her white skirt nervously.

"Oh my bad... you a virgin aren't you?"

"*Mi amor*, leave the poor girl alone." Culebra playfully tapped Yolanda.

"That's not a bad thing, you know." Yolanda whispered.

"I know. I'm just not comfortable talking about *that* in mixed company." Regina whispered back.

"Regina, I don't know you well, *pero*, I know Alejandro and he's a good man. He's gonna need you to help him through this."

"He's right my daughter. Alejandro needs you. You will make a good queen." Queen Anka said in Spanish as she entered the room.

I thought she didn't speak English? Regina thought to herself. She stood and bowed slightly. "Thanks. I will think about it." She replied in Spanish.

"Who's right about what?" Alejandro asked as he came in behind his mother.

"Oh, nothing important." Regina blushed. She felt backed into a corner and she needed to get herself together before she could ever be good for Alejandro. "I talked with my boss about declaring this area as ancestral grounds and with the pictures I took outside the mountain and the burial grounds I saw, it should be no problem."

"That is *fantastico, hermosa!* You're a miracle worker!" Alejandro exclaimed. He then explained to his mother in Spanish what Regina said. She hugged Regina and kissed her cheek.

"See, you will be a great queen!" She whispered in Spanish to Regina.

"Oh by the way, Rosa bought it that you too were dead after I sent her the pictures we took. I also spoke to my uncle. He was pissed that Rosa wanted me dead! He leaked some evidence to the press about Rosa and Javier's illegal activites. That should ruin their standing in legitimate business and he is sending a copy the DEA. Those *perras* will go to jail!" Culebra declared.

"I'm sure with them out of the way, your uncle will make a play for the Hermosillo family to be the new head of the cartel." Alejandro said.

"Hey, the devil you know right? Your home will be protected and you and Regina won't have the cartel on your ass."

"True *hermano*." Alejandro fist bumped Culebra.

"So not to be rude or nothing, but me and my lady are gonna head to the festival. I promised her since she's never been and we're here, you know?"

"Well, since no one is after me, I should be able to go too. I mean, that is the reason I came to Alamos. If that's alright with you, Alex?" Regina asked softly, hoping he would say yes. She didn't want to leave him, but she really needed to get out.

"She can come with us. We'll keep an eye on her." Culebra offered.

"That is a great idea. I will join you, *hermosa*, I could use a break." Alejandro said.

"Are you sure you are up to it?" Regina asked.

"Claro que si. I don't think my father would not want me to sit around being sad. Let's celebrate his life."

Great... She thought to herself. Now she really felt guilty. *He only wants to go because I do.* She just wanted to be away from everything and enjoy the festival like she intended from the beginning before losing her luggage and 'Mr. Sexy Glowing Eyes' walked into her life. She smiled and nodded.

"*Vamos*!" Culebra said.

The *Plaza De Armas* was filled with people from all walks of life enjoying the 36th edition of the *Alfonzo Ortiz Tirado Festival*. Music filled the air and the two couples made their way down the street to the Alameda Stage. The band, *Pata De Palo*, got the crowd moving their hips to the song, *El Cuarto de Tula*.

"*Bailar* baby! Let's get it!" Culebra pulled Yolanda into the crowd of dancers dancing in the center of the plaza and they salsa danced to the beat.

Alejandro took Regina's hand "I believe they have

challenged us. Shall we, *hermosa?*"

"We shall." Regina beamed.

Alejandro spun Regina out and pulled her back in. She loved salsa and she swayed her hips seductively to the beat.

She impressed him with her dancing. *Perfecto!* She seemed to come out of her shyness even more. Regina love to dance more than anything.

Yolanda tapped Culebra and pointed to Alejandro and Regina. "Damn, if she keeps dancing like that, she won't be a virgin for much longer!" Culebra commented.

"Boy stop! Leave that girl alone!" Yolanda laughed.

Culebra spun Yolanda so that her butt was facing him and he gave her a love pat. She twerked and swiveled her hips at the same time.
"That's my woman!" Culebra beat his chest and let out a few "aye ha-ha-ha ayes" as he watched his woman dance.

Alejandro and Regina began to watch Yolanda and cheered her on. "Okay, I think they won! I can't twerk." Regina exclaimed.

"No, *hermosa,* you are a winner and I am the luckiest man here." Alejandro whispered in her ear.

Regina kissed his cheek and smiled, "Your people are

the true winners, you are going to be a great king, Alex."

After they finished dancing, the couples went to the museum to see Regina's portrait of Alejandro in jaguar form.

"It's beautiful, you have a great eye, Regina." Yolanda commented.

"Yes, she does, doesn't she? That's my talented *hermosa*." Alejandro sighed and kissed Regina's cheek

*****

The coronation of King Alejandro took place three days after the funeral. They decorated the whole town like it was Christmas, with lights, wreaths, and cactus flowers. Alejandro's crown was an elaborate headdress with white feathers and the pelt of jaguar skin around the headband worn by the previous kings. He would wear a traditional pelt of jaguar skin loin cloth with white feathers around the waist, no shirt and no shoes.

There was mixture of sadness in the air for the late king and excitement for the new king. Twenty-five women of the tribe prepared a feast for the reception that followed.

Queen Anka gave Regina the native dress she wore at her husband's coronation. As a surprise for Regina, Anka pulled out her crown and instructed the high priest to crown Regina and Alejandro together at the church ceremony, blessing and binding them as a couple in the old tradition in the old language and as king and queen.

It honored Regina to wear the white sleeveless dress with a handmade jaguar pelt overlay and a belt made of white feathers, but she felt strange at the same time. She liked Queen Anka, but missed Mama Izzie and her dog, Chi-Chi. She wanted them to be here. To share her secret of Alejandro and his family. She felt alone despite the smiling faces all around her. The queen set up for Regina's hair to be washed and braided. Much to Regina's surprise, the women moisturized her hair with something that smelled great after washing it and it made her hair soft and shiny.

Alejandro was also feeling nervous. He wanted his father. He felt he wasn't ready to be king, even though he was already leading his people. This ceremony was more of a spiritual one to be blessed by *EL Shalam* as the *anointed* king of the La Avana tribe. He wanted to see Regina. She made plans to return to Arizona after the ceremony. He didn't want to be king, not without *her* as his queen. His mother would be queen until he married. What if he married Regina? No, he knew she wasn't ready for that. She had a life in Arizona. He couldn't expect her to give up her life to rule with him, could he?

Alejandro, dressed in his traditional attire, went to Regina's room, but his mother accosted him and insisted he leave her alone so that he could mentally prepare for the ceremony. She assured him Regina would be available after the ceremony.

Filled to capacity, the jaguar shifters waited for their new king. Two pillows covered in jaguar pelts sat at the altar. Regina was so out of sorts, she didn't notice. Regina sat in the front row next to Queen Anka, who was wearing her crown. Regina looked beautiful, but there was a sadness in her eyes. She explained to the queen how much she missed her mother. Anka hugged her and reassured her she would see them soon. Two rows behind her were Culebra and Yolanda, who was sporting a five-carat diamond on her left hand.

Suddenly everyone stood up and the people began to chant in a language that was not Spanish. A barefoot Alejandro entered the church and everyone remained standing until he reached the altar. Regina thought him handsome and regal despite not wearing jewels or a velvet cape.

The high priest motioned for Regina and Anka to come up. Anka took Regina's hand and led her to the altar. She stood next to Alejandro who looked lovingly at her. Anka stood on her right side. The chanting stopped and the priest began to speak in the same language as the chanting. He removed Anka's crown and Anka stepped back. He then motioned for the couple to kneel on the pillows.

"What's going on?" Regina whispered.

Alejandro answered her with his thoughts. *I don't know, The last coronation was before I was born. Just go with it, hermosa. The priest knows what he is doing.*

The priest may have known what he was doing, but she didn't and the fact that Alejandro didn't know either, made her feel worse. This was not right. Something was off. However, not wanting to embarrass herself in front of Alejandro's tribe, she kept quiet.

The priest joined their hands and said a blessing of sorts in an ancient language. Regina felt a warm sensation through her body that almost made her dizzy. A rush of power flowed to her from Alejandro. Then the priest took Alejandro's crown headdress from a near by table and placed it on Alejandro's head. He placed his hands on

Alejandro's shoulders and said another blessing. The tribe began chanting again and then stopped. The priest did the same with Regina, placing Anka's crown on her head and a jaguar pelt robe around her neck.

Suddenly, Regina realized in that moment that she had just become the queen of the tribe, albeit in a spiritual sense, but still a queen.

Mierda! Is this fool really going to act like he doesn't know what's happening? Was he marrying her without even asking her first? Regina's mind raced as the tribe chanted again.

After the chanting ended, the priest motioned for the couple to rise and face the tribe. Everyone cheered and Alejandro, still holding on to Regina's hand, led her down the aisle and out of the church.

"*Lo siento, hermosa.* I didn't know this was going to happen."

Regina pulled her hand away. "Really? What? No vision beforehand, or did you have one and forget to tell me? Are we married? I mean, you haven't even asked me!"

"No *hermosa*, that was not a wedding ceremony."

"So what the hell was it?"

"You are my divine anointed queen and ruler of my people. At least from what I understood of the ceremony. I shared my power with you and my mother gave you her crown. She is no longer the queen, you are."

"No one asked me if *I* wanted to be queen! I am going back to Arizona, I can't be queen!" The panic in her voice made it go up an octave.

Alejandro pulled her to him. "*Tranquila, mi hermosa.* We have blessed you to rule this tribe, a gift from my mother and *EL Shalam*. I love that she approves of you and if she did not believe you would be a good queen, she would not have given up her crown. But yes, she should have discussed this with us. You do have a choice to rule or not."

Tears filled Regina's eyes. It was too much, too soon. "I'm so sorry, Alejandro. You are amazing and I love your family, your village. It is a wonderful gift, but I am not worthy." She took off the crown and robe and handed them back to Alejandro. Then she ran back to the main house to change. Dark clouds suddenly formed in the sky.

"*Hermosa, por favor*! *Hermosa*! Regina don't do this! I cannot do this without you!"

Alejandro's eyes glowed as lightening flashed and rain

fell hard on the ground. Alejandro went after Regina when his mother stopped him.

"Let her go, son. She will come back." Anka said in Spanish.

Tears welled and threatened to fall from his eyes. Alejandro took off his crown and robe and giving both crowns and robes to his mother, he stripped off his loincloth and shifted into his jaguar form and ran away. Culebra and Yolanda came out of the church.

"Should I go after him?" Culebra asked.

"No, they'll sort it out." Yolanda said.

Epilogue

Two months passed. Javier and Rosa Carrillo have been indicted and are in U.S. Federal custody. Rosa lost her seat on the board of the *Groupo Susteno* Food Company for violating the moral clause in her contract by using the bakery in Southern Sonora as a front for drug trafficking.

Mesa Esmeralda as well as the land surrounding it have been declared as sacred ancestral grounds thanks to Regina's contacts with the ACC, partnering with Mexico's primary federal environmental agency, SEMARNAP, the U.S. EPA , the Mexican protection of environment (PROFEPA), and some 'unofficial' help from the Hermosillo family to speed up the process. *Groupo Susteno* were forced to pull up stakes in Alamos, Sonora in order to avoid charges against them because of Rosa Carrillo.

The Jaguars as well as other animals who live in the

region and the unique flora and fauna became protected by Mexican Wildlife Conservation making it illegal to hunt or build manufacturing plants that would otherwise disturb or disrupt the species in that region.

Culebra and Yolanda eloped in San Carlos and are now expecting their first child in December. They travel between their home in Puerto Vallarta and the Aztecas tribal home in Nuevo Guaymas - San Carlos.

Juan Pablo Hermosillo and the Hermosillo family is head of what is now called the Hermosillo Cartel. He has honored the peace agreement between the tribes and the Sonoran desert in Sonora. Sonora and it's surrounding cities are off limits to drug and human trafficking. Enforced by the joint task force of the Federales, DEA, Border Patrol and 'unofficially' the Hermosillo and Hernandez families in Durango who organized private security made up of one hundred members of the La Avana and Aztecas shifter tribes.

Regina returned to Tucson, Arizona where she continued to work for the ACC and with her Mama Izzie at the family veterinarian clinic on the weekends. She has tried to forget Alejandro, but she cannot. Her chihuahua, Chi-Chi, tells her every day to go to him. Even Mama Izzie, to whom Regina confided and swore to secrecy, tried to talk her into to going back. Her ability to speak to animals has increased, she can talk to all animals now and every where she goes, they talk to her.

Regina sat on her couch in sweatpants and a crop tee folding clothes watching the news while Chi-Chi sat at her feet.

"In other news today... an unusual sighting of a large male jaguar in the Santa Catalina mountains. Residents in the area are calling him, "*El Jefe*" and say he has been there for the past two months and appears to be alone as the nearest jaguar pride is four hundred and seventy-five miles away in Sonora Mexico..."

Alejandro. Regina thought to herself. Was he looking for her?

It's him, oh I knew he would come for you!

"I think you are right, Chi-Chi, but why would he leave his tribe?"

A knock on the door brought her out of her thoughts. She opened the door to see... Alejandro. He was impeccably dressed in brown pants, a crisp white shirt with a brown blazer. She on the hand, was very casual in a green crop tee, gray sweat pants and bare feet. Her curly hair in a messy bun on the top of the head.

Alejandro smiled at her as if she were the most beautiful woman in the world. *His* woman. The one he spent the last two months searching for. He bowed deeply, "*Mi hermosa reina.* (My beautiful queen)." He stood up and reached into his blazer pocket and took out a small box. He opened it to reveal a 14k white gold art deco designed two carat oval cut diamond ring with halo and three additional emerald cut diamonds on each side. He knelt down and raised the box to her. "Will you marry me, my queen?"

Regina gasped as Chi-Chi came and sat by her side. "Yes, I will, my king."

Alejandro stood and placed the ring on Regina's finger, kissing her forehead. She admired the ring briefly before wrapping her arms around him and hugging him tightly.

Chi-Chi began to bark and run happily around them in circles.

"Who is this pretty lady?" Alejandro asked.

"This is Chi-Chi. Chi-Chi, this is Alejandro."

He is even better looking than you described!

"I think she likes you." Regina smiled.

Alejandro released Regina and picked up Chi-Chi, petting her softly. Chi-Chi barked.

"She says welcome to the family!" Regina beamed.

"And welcome to mine, Chi-Chi." Alejandro said as he placed her back on the floor. He picked Regina up and kissed her deeply before carrying her to her bedroom where he set her down gently. He moved from her mouth to her neck kissing and licking it softly and she moaned. "Do not run from me again," he said with a low growl.

"Never," Regina breathed. Her body was throbbing and she felt flushed from the power that surged from Alejandro.

He reached under her tee to find her braless. He caressed her breasts, one at a time and flicked his fingertips over her swollen nipples. Another moan from her from caused his member to throb mercilessly against his pants. He pulled her t-shirt over her head and threw them in the corner. He began to kiss her breast as he eased her onto the bed. He quickly undressed as he watched her lying in wait for him. Naked, he climbed on the bed and continued his assault of kisses down to her belly. He slid off her sweatpants and panties, taking in her scent. Sliding her legs open, he kissed the inside of her thighs, working to the spot he wanted to taste.

Stopping at her moist center, a low growl escaped him. Her sex reminded him of a delicate orchid. He lowered his head to her center and sucked on the swollen bud. Regina gasped. He wrapped his arms around her thighs and pulled her closer to his face claiming her with his tongue. Regina's hips began to buck as the first wave of an orgasm descended and she trembled, spilling her essence. It felt amazing. Alejandro drank and licked every drop.

Regina sat up, suddenly embarrassed, she thought she urinated on him. "Oh my god, I am so sorry."

"For what *hermosa*?"

" I wet the bed." She said shyly.

Alejandro laughed softly. "Not in the way you think, *hermosa*. You have nothing to be ashamed of. You ejaculated."

Regina could not help but giggle at the way he said, "ejaculated".You mean that's supposed to happen?"

"Yes."

"How do you know that if you are a virgin?"

"My father taught me many things, *hermosa*. One of which, is how to please a woman. It was an embarrassing anatomy lesson, but one I am glad I learned."

"Me too," she whispered.

Alejandro crawled up to her and kissed her gently then deeply, easing her back onto the bed. "Are you ready to be mine forever?"

"Yes," she breathed.

Alejandro's eyes began to glow as he gazed lovingly at her. He guided his member and entered slowly. She was very tight, gripping him like a glove as he sank deeper into her. He was not prepared to feel this good and he fought not to hurt her. She became more wet as he eased in and out.

Regina gasped and moaned. It was not as painful as she thought it would be. She opened her legs wider and pressed her hips against him. He began to thrust faster as his power began to flow over her. She felt so good he could barely stand it. The pleasure was too much and after a few moments, he roared, climaxing and releasing powerfully inside her. Before they could catch their breath, a vision played in both their minds.

Regina looked to be about five or six months pregnant. She and Alejandro were walking with a little boy who looked like Alejandro when he was three years old, walking between them. They were headed to the center of the town square where everyone was gathered. There was food and music. Mama Izzie and Anka were chatting and turned to wave at them. Then the vision stopped.

"Was that...?" Regina began.

"A vision, yes. Did you see it too, *hermosa*?" He looked down at Regina, whose dark brown eyes began to glow softly.

"That was amazing! What does it mean?" Regina exclaimed.

"It means we better have the wedding soon, *hermosa*, before you give birth to our son." Alejandro laughed.

"Sure, but first, let's practice some more for the honeymoon. I think I am getting the hang of it."

"As you wish, *mi hermosa reina*."

*****

Thank you for reading
Passion's Pride Alejandro

This story is based on real facts about the Sonoran desert which is approximately 100,000 square miles, and spans across southern Arizona, southeastern California, the Baja California Peninsula, the islands in the Gulf of California and Sonora, Mexico. As well as being home to an abundance of foliage, this desert, like most, also contains cacti unlike other deserts in the United States, the Sonoran Desert gets occasional snowfall in the winter time, a very unique characteristic. All in all, the Sonoran desert's wide variety of terrain and weather makes it a desirable habitat for many animals and plants.

Endangered Species

Jaguars are rarely seen in the United States of America due to human interference. There are reportedly around 50-120 in the Sonoran Desert with eye-witness accounts proving their presence. Jaguars are hunted primarily for their beautiful coat, and also have become endangered due to habitat loss.

The extinction of the Jaguar within the Sonoran Desert would result in the major consumer reduction. The Jaguar is possibly the biggest predator within the Sonoran area and ensure that larger animals like the big horn sheep do not overpopulate and consume all of the producers.

You can find more books by Mahogany SilverRain at https://www.mahoganysilverrain.net
Passion's Pride Alejandro is book two of the Passion's Pride Series.

Other books by Mahogany SilverRain:

The Grand Dame of Bourbon Street, A Dominique LeRoy Novel

Love Bytes A Vampire's Tale

Tell Me You Love Me, Kenya Clark Series Book One

The Rise of Lucious Morningside, Kenya Clark Series Book Two

Passion's Pride Leonessa, Book One

Shanghai Sheena

Riona's Luck

A Slave's Heart

Winter's Kiss

Imani's Gift

Sake and Pumpkin Pie

Ebony Encounters: A Trilogy of Erotic Tales

www.ingramcontent.com/pod-product-compliance
Lightning Source LLC
Chambersburg PA
CBHW070520130626
46555CB00003B/1294